Nicola C...............he

DEALING
WITH
FEELINGS

It's my turn

Natasha waits patiently while
Dad makes dinner.

Natasha takes turns when playing cards.

Natasha waits for
her turn to talk
to Grandma.

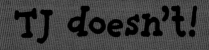

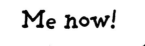

Natasha waits until the bath is ready.

Natasha waits for Mum to help squeeze the toothpaste.

Natasha waits for her bedtime story.

But there's
one thing Natasha
can't wait for...

It's my Turn

Introduction

Younger children often find it almost impossible to wait and take turns. In this book, Natasha has learned to wait and let others go first, but her younger brother TJ hasn't! He is still at the stage where impulse rules, and sometimes Natasha's patience seems to be overlooked. However, when goodnight kisses are on offer, Natasha is just as impatient as her little brother!

Top tips for using this book

Remember that you don't need to do them all, or all at once!

1 Read the book several times so your child is familiar with the story. Talk about younger children at home or at nursery who haven't learned to take turns or wait. Talk about how they will learn as they grow up. Remember that your child may still find this difficult too!

2 Play a simple card game or do a puzzle together, using a teddy or soft toy to keep butting in and saying, 'My turn, my turn!' Ask your child how s/he feels when this happens, and what s/he could say to the teddy to help him be patient. Help your child to use words for feelings, such as cross, irritated, unkind, mean, bored, as well as patient, kind or friendly.

3 Play plenty of card and board games with your child, practising taking turns and thanking him/her when s/he shows patience. Don't make the game go on too long. Praise your child for managing disappointment if he or she doesn't win. Remember, this is difficult for small children. If you have enough people, play these games in pairs so you can talk about how you feel if you have to wait for others, or how you feel about not winning.

4 Teach your child some strategies for waiting, such as counting to ten, playing a finger game, or singing a waiting song that recognises the difficulty, such as:

> *I am waiting, I am waiting,*
> *Waiting here, waiting here,*
> *I am being patient, I am being patient,*
> *Look at me! Look at me!*

5 Show your child good examples of waiting – control your own behaviour and body language if you have to wait in a queue, or in traffic, or for someone older or slower than you. Children learn a lot from watching you!

6 Don't forget to thank older or more mature children for waiting and taking turns. This will reinforce the behaviour, and your words will not be lost on younger siblings.

Published 2014 by Featherstone Education
An imprint of Bloomsbury Publishing Plc
50 Bedford Square, London, WC1B 3DP
www.bloomsbury.com

Bloomsbury is a registered trademark of Bloomsbury Publishing Plc

ISBN 978-1-4729-0774-5

Text © Nicola Call and Sally Featherstone
Illustrations © Melissa Four

A CIP record for this publication is available from
the British Library.

Printed in China by Leo Paper Products, Heshan, Guangdong

This book is produced using paper that is made
from wood grown in managed, sustainable forests.
It is natural, renewable and recyclable. The logging
and manufacturing process conform to the
environmental regulations of the country of origin.

10 9 8 7 6 5 4 3 2 1